Ellie's New Home

J FIC Citra

Citra, B.
Ellie's new home.

PRICE: $4.85 (jf/d)

AN
ORCA
YOUNG
READER

Ellie's New Home
BECKY CITRA

ORCA BOOK PUBLISHERS

Library and Archives Canada Cataloguing in Publication

Citra, Becky.
Ellie's new home

ISBN 1-55143-164-5

1. Immigrants—Canada—Juvenile fiction. I. Title.
PS8555.I87E44 1999   jC813'.54   C99-910903-0
PZ7.C499E1 1999

First Published in the United States: 1999

Library of Congress Catalog Card Number: 99-65483

Free teachers' guide available at www.orcabook.com

Orca Book Publishers gratefully acknowledges the support for its publishing programs provided by the following agencies: the Government of Canada through the Book Publishing Industry Development Program and the Canada Council for the Arts, and the Province of British Columbia through the BC Arts Council and the Book Publishing Tax Credit.

Cover design by Christine Toller
Cover and interior illustrations by Don Kilby

ORCA BOOK PUBLISHERS   ORCA BOOK PUBLISHERS
PO Box 5626, STN. B   PO Box 468
VICTORIA, BC CANADA   CUSTER, WA USA
V8R 6S4   98240-0468

www.orcabook.com

09 08 07 06 • 7 6 5 4

Printed and bound in Canada

To my mother

Chapter 1
Grandmother's House

"Ellie ..."

I frowned at my little brother. "Be quiet, Max."

Max and I crouched on the landing of the long staircase. Far away in the big, dark house, one of Grandmother's clocks struck the hour. The winter wind rattled against the windows.

Papa and Grandmother had been downstairs in the parlor since supper. They were having a terrible argument.

I leaned over the stairs. I heard Papa say, "I can't think of one good reason why Ellie shouldn't go."

"She's too young," said Grandmother. I couldn't see her, but I could imagine her face — her mouth a thin, straight line and her eyes boring into Papa's like hot coals.

"Nonsense," said Papa. "She's nine years old."

Thud, thud, thud went Papa's boots, back and forth across the parlor floor. I knew that meant Papa was thinking.

"She's not strong," said Grandmother.

"She'll get strong," said Papa.

Grandmother snorted. "She'll get sick. And then what will you do? The wilderness is no place for a girl."

I frowned. I wrapped my arms around my legs. What were Papa and Grandmother talking about? And why did Grandmother sound so angry?

Thud, thud, thud. Papa was thinking hard.

"There will be no schools or churches," said Grandmother. "How can you even consider such a thing?"

Papa stopped pacing. "They are building schools and churches," he said in his stubborn voice.

"Humph," said Grandmother.

I heard the creak of the tea trolley wheels and the swish of Clarissa's apron. Clarissa was Grandmother's kitchen maid. She had a round, red face like a plum.

Teacups clinked. After a few minutes, Grandmother said, "That will be all for tonight, Clarissa."

"Yes, ma'am."

I dug my fingers into the thick carpet. And then I heard Grandmother say in a tight voice, "And Max?"

"Max too," said Papa softly.

Beside me, Max stopped wiggling and

sat very still. I slipped my hand over his.

"Max is *five*," said Grandmother. "He's a baby."

"Ellie will look after him." Papa's voice rose. "They need to see things. They need to play with other children. They're alone too much."

Grandmother sniffed. "Heathen children. That's all you'll find there. Quite unsuitable."

What did heathen mean? Grandmother made it sound terrible. I shivered. Where was this place with heathen children and wilderness and no schools or churches? And why did Papa want to go so badly?

"You are making a big mistake," said Grandmother.

"No," said Papa. "I love Ellie and Max. I must take them. I would miss them too much."

I held my breath. I waited for Grandmother to say, "I love them too, and I will miss them."

But Grandmother said nothing.

"That settles it then," said Papa. He sounded sad and excited at the same time. "My children are coming to Canada with me."

Chapter 2
The Family

I perched on the edge of the wagon seat.

Sometimes the wagon swayed back and forth like the huge ship we had sailed on from England.

Sometimes it bumped and bounced in the ruts, making Papa grunt and the horses swish their tails.

I was too excited to mind. We had

left the inn in the town early in the morning. Papa said we were close to our homestead. I pressed my hands against my knees. It was hard not to shout out loud.

It was early summer in 1835. Papa and Max and I had sailed from England in the spring. We landed in Montreal, where we bought the wagon and our horses, Billy and George. I liked traveling with Papa. But I couldn't wait to see my new home.

When Papa stopped the wagon in a grove of trees, Max said, "Are we here?"

Papa shook his head. "Not yet."

I could see a cabin with a curl of smoke, which meant someone was already living on this land. Our land would be just trees. Billy and George would help clear the fields and Papa would build our house.

A man with a long black beard was chopping wood. A small boy with an armful of sticks stared at us. He had bright eyes and a pointed face like a fox.

"Hello," called Papa. He jumped down

from the wagon.

Papa and the man talked while Max and I waited in the wagon. Then Papa told us to jump down too. The man showed Papa a log corral for Billy and George. He brought buckets of water and oats.

Max helped the boy gather kindling and carry it into the cabin. A girl came outside and scattered yellow corn from a pan. A flurry of brown chickens scurried from the side of the cabin. Their heads bobbed up and down like puppets. I said shyly, "Do they have names?"

The girl looked surprised. "They're only chickens."

She scattered a few more handfuls of corn and then said gruffly, "Here. You take a turn."

I took the pan and shook it gently. A fat brown hen rushed towards my feet. It snapped its beak and glared at me with angry black eyes.

I dropped the pan and screamed.

A look of amazement swept over the

girl's face. Then she laughed. "Haven't you ever seen chickens before?"

"Only dead ones," I whispered. My cheeks felt hot. "They were hanging in the market when I went shopping with Papa."

The girl's mouth dropped open. Then she shrugged and picked up the pan.

A woman came to the door of the cabin. She was wearing a big blue apron and she had a round red face. I thought right away of Clarissa. The woman banged on a pot with a spoon.

"Come along," said the man. I couldn't see his mouth, but when he talked, his beard bobbed up and down.

Inside the cabin, Max clung to my hand while I peered around curiously. It was dark with log walls and two small windows. Why, I thought, the whole thing would fit into one of Grandmother's rooms. The floor and the table and chairs were made of boards. A curtain hung at one end, and there was a door that led to a tiny bedroom.

The woman was leaning over a pot, which hung in a huge stone fireplace.

Papa said, "This is my daughter, Ellie. And this — "

"I am Max," said Max in a loud voice.

The woman smiled. "It is nice to meet you, Max. And Ellie."

We sat at the table, Papa between Max and I. The woman brought bowls of stew and warm cornbread. Then we bowed our heads. The man said, "Bless our food and our home. Keep these travelers safe."

"Amen," said the girl and the boy.

I wondered what Grandmother would think if she could hear them. I had asked Clarissa about that word heathen. Clarissa had told me that a heathen was a person who didn't know God. It was no wonder Grandmother was so against our trip to Canada.

After the meal, Papa pulled out his pipe. He told the family stories of our journey from England.

I tried to sit up straight in my chair

the way Grandmother had taught me. But my shoulders slumped. I felt like something heavy was pressing on my eyes. I swallowed a huge yawn.

"And what do you think of Canada so far, Ellie?" said the woman.

I jumped. Everyone was staring at me. My face felt hot. I wanted to say, "I don't know." But Papa didn't like it when I said that. He said that I must try harder to think of things to say when people talked to me.

"It is big," Max squeaked.

The man and the woman laughed. Papa laughed too. And then he chided gently, "You mustn't interrupt, Max." He looked at me.

"Canada is fine," I mumbled.

My face felt even hotter. I wished I had said something smart like, Canada is beautiful. The water is so blue and the forests go forever. I wished I had told them about the deer and her fawn that had watched us that morning from a grove of trees.

But it was too late. Papa and the man were talking about deeds for land, and the woman and the girl were clearing the dishes from the table.

Once Papa glanced at me and frowned slightly. He wanted me to help. But I felt too shy to move. So I pretended that I was listening to the man, and when the girl came close to me, I didn't look at her.

Chapter 3
It's Hard to be Brave

"Tell me about our new home, Papa," I said.

I was sitting on the cabin step, leaning against Papa's knees. It was night and the trees looked like thin, black shadows. An owl hooted in the darkness. Through the open doorway, I could hear Max talking to the woman, his voice prattling on like

Grandmother's milkman in England.

Papa pretended to think. "Let's see, it will be a little bit like this cabin, built out of logs."

"But you said it will have a painted floor," I reminded him. "And we'll have big windows that let the sun in, right, Papa?"

"Right, little sparrow."

"Will you build our cabin right away, Papa?" I asked. I knew I sounded as impatient as Max, but I was too excited to care.

Papa tapped the end of my nose. "Not right away. I will have to clear some land first. For a while we will live in a shanty, which is like a little cabin."

I snuggled closer to Papa. "I wish we could keep going tonight."

Papa gazed silently at the dark forest. He said in a soft voice, "You were a little girl when Mama died and you were very brave."

I was quiet. Sometimes it was hard to remember Mama.

"And you were very, very brave when

you said goodbye to Grandmother in England."

I traced my finger along the edge of the step. What was Papa saying? I wasn't brave at all, and Papa knew it. I was afraid of the man who brought the vegetables and loud noises and the doctor who had come to see Mama.

Papa touched my shoulder. "You must be brave one more time."

Papa spoke quickly now. He didn't look at me. "I want you and Max to stay here with this family while I go ahead. It won't be for long. I'll come back for you as soon as I get settled on our land."

My chest felt like it was being squeezed. "No!"

"It will only be for a little while. Max can play with the boy. It will be fun for him." Papa tried to smile. "The girl is your age. You can be friends."

"But I don't like her."

Papa frowned.

My voice became small. "She's bossy.

And she stares at me. Please, Papa."

"I'm sorry," said Papa.

My heart thumped wildly. It hurt to breathe. "You can't leave us! We won't be any trouble, I promise!"

"You need to be with a family, and I need some time to settle our affairs." Papa's face closed. "Besides, Ellen, I have made the arrangements already."

Papa didn't say little sparrow. He didn't say Ellie. He said Ellen. I bent my head. My heart felt like a small, cold stone.

I hated the fat woman, who must have told Papa to do this. I hated the man with the gloomy beard and the sharp-eyed boy and girl. And for one terrible minute, I hated Papa too.

I knew I must not argue.

But how could Papa leave us?

That night I crawled under a quilt beside the girl. The mattress was thin and filled with something prickly. Max and the boy slept on another mattress beside us. Firelight flickered around the edges of the curtain wall. I could hear the murmur of the grownups' voices, Papa's up and down like the wind.

The girl had skinny chicken legs. I stiffened my back so I wouldn't touch them.

The boy with the fox face whispered in the darkness, "If your papa leaves, are you orphans?"

"No, stupid," said the girl. "He's still their papa, isn't he? He's coming back."

I tried to swallow. My throat filled with a hard lump.

I felt the girl touch the edge of my nightie. "Is that lace? Is your papa rich?"

The boy giggled.

I could feel the girl's hot breath on my cheek. "Did you have a very best friend in England?"

My nose prickled. My eyes ached with tears. I squeezed them shut and kept very still.

"I've never had a best friend," said the girl.

I thought, Go away! Go away!

After a few minutes, the girl said, "Oh, well then." She made a clicking sound with her tongue and rolled over.

When I woke in the morning, the girl was gone. A round lump pressed against my stomach. It was Max. He was sucking his thumb, making snuffling noises. He sounded like the funny tame squirrel that lived outside Grandmother's kitchen window. I crawled out of bed and pushed back the curtain. The woman was leaning over a pot in the fireplace, stirring.

I ran to the door. My stomach felt hollow. There was no wagon. There were no Billy and George. The road stretched like a brown ribbon into the forest.

Papa was gone.

Chapter 4
Breakfast

"Ma, she's playing with her food!"

"I'm not," I said. I looked down at my bowl of milk porridge.

"Watch your tongue, Mary," said the man. His voice rumbled like a train inside his beard. "Ellie is our guest."

The little boy snorted. Two red spots burned in Mary's cheeks. It serves her right, I thought.

The man stood up. He reached for his hat on a peg by the door. "Trevor, you boys can play for a while, but then I'll need you in the field. Mary, you see that you mind Ma."

He shut the door with a bang. Mary glanced at Ma's wide back. Then she stuck out her tongue at the closed door. I sucked in my breath. Mary's pa looked so fierce.

"Manners, Mary," said Ma.

I thought that Ma must have eyes in the back of her head. I stared at her. She was the fattest person I had ever seen. When she moved around the cabin, she was like the ship we had sailed on from England. I sighed and stirred my porridge. I pushed down a mouthful. I didn't want Mary to say I was staring at Ma.

The porridge tasted plain. I can't eat this, I thought. I peeked at Max. His cheeks were pale. A thin line of milk dribbled down his chin. I felt my eyes prickle with tears.

Ma set a jug of molasses on the table. It smelled a little like the brown sugar in the metal cannister in Grandmother's kitchen. I poured some on my porridge. It sloshed out too fast, making a puddle and then a dark lake in the middle of my bowl.

"Ma," said Mary, "she's wasting molasses."

The molasses smelled horrible now, sweet and syrupy. I closed my eyes. I felt dizzy.

Ma whisked the sticky, messy bowl away. "Your tummy must be all in a whirl," she said in a kind voice. "You can tell me later when you get hungry."

I opened my eyes in surprise. Mary slid a sharp sideways look at Trevor. Her look said, What a baby! I bit my lip. Mary was mean. I wasn't at all sorry I had said those things about her to Papa.

After breakfast we went outside. There were black stumps everywhere and one big cherry tree. Max and I sat on stumps in front of the cabin. I had the idea that we would keep sitting there until Papa came back. After a minute, Mary sat down beside us. Trevor climbed up into the branches of the tree.

I looked around. The sky was like a blue bowl. A thin yellow dog lay panting in a patch of shade. Red chickens scratched in the dirt. On the other side of the road was a log fence and a field of green grass. Past that, across another fence, I could see the slow-moving figure of Mary's pa and a pair of plodding work horses.

"Hey!" cried Trevor. "Look at me!"

He crouched on a thick limb, high up in the tree. He flapped his arms. He jumped and landed on the dusty ground with a thud.

Trevor stood up. He dusted off his knees. "Can you do that?"

"What?" I said.

"Can you fly like a bird like me?"

My heart thumped. The truth was, I

didn't know. I had never tried. In Grandmother's house, nobody jumped. "I could," I said stiffly, "if I wanted to. But I don't want to."

"Humph," said Mary.

"I do," said Max. "I want to fly like a bird."

"No, Max!" I said in a sharp voice.

The yellow dog raised his head. He barked. Trevor and Mary stopped looking at me. They stared up the road. A horse whinnied. Wagon wheels creaked.

I stood up. My heart thumped hard. "Papa's come back!" I cried.

Chapter 5
She's a Liar!

A wagon driven by a tall, thin woman rumbled around a bend in the road.

"It's Mrs. Robertson," said Mary. "She doesn't have a husband. She comes to see Ma."

I sank down on the stump. The wagon creaked to a stop.

"Good morning, Mary. Good morning,

Trevor," said Mrs. Robertson. She stepped out of the wagon. "Trevor, be a good boy and look after Ben for me."

Mary said, "This is Ellie from England. And Max."

Mrs. Robertson smiled. Her teeth were big. She smelled like horses. When she had gone inside, Mary said, "Now we'll get to have tea. Ma saves it for company."

Mary leaned closer to me. "Mrs. Robertson is a widow," she whispered. "She talked her poor husband to death. It's true, even though Ma gets mad when you say it. And everyone knows she's looking for a new husband."

Mary gave me a sly look. "Maybe Mrs. Robertson will marry your papa."

I clenched my hands into fists. Mary was a stupid girl. She said stupid things. I was glad when Ma called us to come inside.

Ma sliced a round, dark, plum cake. She set out a teapot decorated with pink roses and pale green leaves, and matching tea-cups. She poured cups of hot, weak tea.

I sipped my tea slowly. I could feel Mrs. Robertson staring at me. I tried to think of something to say. "We had tea every day in England. And little cakes with pink icing. Didn't we, Max?"

"I don't know," said Max through a mouthful of plum cake.

"We did." I could hear my voice getting louder. "Don't you remember Clarissa and her tea trolley?"

Mary's eyes flashed. But Mrs. Robertson laughed loudly, showing all her teeth. "I should think you'll be missing a lot more than fancy cakes and tea trolleys."

Mrs. Robertson raised her eyebrows at Ma. They were bushy with hairs growing straight up. Mary was wrong. Papa would *never* marry her!

"I hope the children's father knew what he was doing when he headed off into the wilderness without them," she said.

Ma frowned, but Mrs. Robertson went on. "It's as easy as apple pie to get yourself lost."

I sucked in my breath. What was Mrs. Robertson saying? Papa would never get lost!

"I've heard of many settlers who left behind part of their family and never did find them again." Mrs. Robertson waggled her eyebrows again. "*Many* settlers. Why — "

Crash!

The pink rosebud teacup slid from my fingers. It smashed on the cabin floor.

"Mercy," said Mrs. Robertson. "The girl's as white as a sheet."

I stared at the broken cup. Mrs. Robertson was a liar! A liar! Papa was coming back. He had promised!

From far away, I heard Ma say, "You've frightened her with your talk." And then, "Don't cry, Ellie. It's just a teacup."

"It's not just a teacup, Ma," said Mary. "It's the rosebud set you brought all the way from Scotland."

Mrs. Robertson's face tightened with disapproval.

I hugged my arms to my chest.

"I never — " Mrs. Robertson started to say.

Ma reached for me. I pushed her away. Max stared at us, his eyes like round black pebbles. I lunged outside and slammed the cabin door.

Chapter 6
A Surprise in the Barn

I crouched in a corner of the barn. A pointed face peered at me from behind a bucket. It had quivering whiskers and tiny, frightened eyes. A mouse! I held my breath.

The barn door creaked. Sun streamed across the floor. The mouse scurried into a pile of sacks.

Ma stood in the middle of the barn.

"Ellie," she said.

I squeezed myself into a little ball. I tried to take tiny breaths. I could hear my heart thumping.

Ma stood very still. She looked like a mountain covered in blue and white flowers.

"Ellie."

I pretended I was the mouse. I pretended I was buried under the pile of sacks.

"Are you here, Ellie?"

Go away!

I was surprised Ma didn't hear me, the words were so loud in my head.

Go away! Go away!

Ma sighed and left. My legs hurt. I stood up and brushed away a few wisps of hay.

I frowned. When Ma didn't find me, she would come back to the barn. I needed a better hiding place. I looked around uncertainly. There was a stall with a wooden door at one end of the barn. I hesitated.

Then I undid the latch and pulled the door open. The stall was cool and shadowy. The floor was covered in a thick layer of straw.

Something pounced through the air. And tumbled back into the straw. Something small and black and fluffy.

"Oh!" I cried. I stepped back.

A fuzzy brown ball scooted towards me, humping its back and taking tiny bouncy jumps.

Kittens! I sucked in my breath. I slid into the stall and closed the door. I knelt down.

The straw was full of wiggly little balls. I counted. One, two, three, four ... no, five kittens. I put out my hand and touched a tiny head.

In England I had a cat for one whole day. The milkman gave it to me. I hid it in my bedroom and Clarissa brought a saucer and cream and some meat scraps. Then Grandmother found it and took it away. She said cats scratched and were dirty and had fleas.

I cupped my hand and picked up one of the tiny kittens. It was black with a snowy white chest and a tiny pink nose.

My hand was filled with a soft, throbbing ball. A pink sliver of tongue shot out and licked my finger. The kitten's tongue felt cool and rough, like Papa's chin when he didn't shave.

I picked up each kitten and cradled it in my hand until I heard its soft purr.

Then I sat right down in the straw and stuck out my legs. One of the kittens tried to scramble over. He dug his tiny claws into my stocking.

Whump! He flopped over on his back.

Then he gave one huge pounce and landed on my shoe. He grabbed the lace and made little growling sounds deep in his throat.

I couldn't help laughing. I scooped him up and held him gently. He was brown with black stripes and a perfect black circle around one eye.

"I'm going to call you Pirate," I said.

I forgot about hiding from Ma. I forgot about Mrs. Robertson. I was too busy playing with the kittens. Pirate was my favorite. He was such an explorer. I buried him in a pile of straw. He kept himself very still for a minute and then exploded like a cannon. Bits of straw dangled from his nose.

"Me-ow!" Pirate pounced on the black kitten's back, and they rolled over and over.

I'll come every day, I thought happily. I'll come every day to see the kittens until Papa gets back.

Then I heard the barn door creak. I heard quick footsteps.

I froze. I tried not to breathe.

The footsteps stopped. I heard Mary's sharp voice. "Those kittens are mine. You can't have them — not even one!"

Chapter 7
Wild Animals

"I don't want one," I said.

I stood up. Mary was blocking the door. I shrank against the side of the stall.

Mary was holding a small tin jug. She knelt down and poured creamy milk into a bowl. The kittens mewed and squeaked. They tumbled over each other to get to the bowl.

Mary gave a satisfied smile. "Their mother

Patsy was eaten by a fox. So I'm their mother now."

A fox! How could Mary sound so calm? I bit my lip. I watched the kittens. They made tiny lapping noises and their tails twitched back and forth. They drank until their chins were white and their tummies were round plump balls. Then three of the kittens curled up in the straw and began to purr. Pirate pounced on the little black kitten's tail. The two rolled over in a squealing ball.

Mary laughed.

Without thinking, I said, "I named him Pirate."

Mary was silent. Her freckles looked like yellow polka dots on her pale cheeks. Then she said in a cross voice, "I haven't given them names yet." She pulled Pirate away from the black kitten. "Mind your manners, you bad thing." I thought Mary sounded like her pa when he scolded her.

Mary rubbed the black kitten between his ears. She picked up the jug. "I have to get back now. Ma wants me to pick berries." She sighed. "You'd better come too. After all, it's not fair if I have to do all the work."

Ma gave us a bucket. We walked along a trail that climbed up a wooded hillside behind the cabin. It was cooler in the trees. Patches of sun and shade lay across the ground like stripes on a zebra. I thought about the fox that ate the mother cat Patsy. I stayed close to Mary and tried not to look into the cool green shadows.

"The best strawberries are at the top," said Mary.

We climbed the hill slowly, then stopped to catch our breath. We sat on a fallen log and Mary drew letters in the dirt with a stick.

Suddenly there was a cracking sound in the bushes. Leaves rustled.

Mary stopped drawing. We both stared

hard at the trees.

"It might be wolves," said Mary. She sounded excited. "Are there wolves in England?"

I swallowed. "No."

"I didn't think so."

A branch snapped. My heart thumped. I could hear Mary breathing heavily beside me.

Mary whispered, "Wolves ... or a bear. These woods are full of wild animals."

My legs felt watery. I tried to shut out Mary's voice. It wasn't true. She was just being mean again.

Then a deer darted into the open. It stared at us with its huge dark eyes. It was so close I could see its black nose quivering. It bounded across the trail and disappeared into the forest.

"Oh," I said, weak with relief.

Mary stood up. "Come on," she said crossly.

We climbed for a few more minutes and then came out into the sunshine. I could see a long way. I could see miles of forest with bits of the brown road showing.

In one direction was the town where Papa had bought supplies. Somewhere in the other direction was our homestead. I was glad I had come now. I thought that if I stayed there long enough, I might even see Papa coming back.

We picked strawberries in the hot sun. Plink plink plink. The bucket filled slowly. After that, we sat on a smooth, warm rock and ate some of the berries. They were the sweetest things I had ever tasted. My fingers turned red and sticky.

Suddenly Mary jumped up. She said, "You carry the bucket first and then I'll take a turn."

Mary walked quickly. Then she began to run down the hill. She ran as fast as the deer. One minute I could see Mary's yellow dress flashing through the trees. Then she was gone.

My heart thudded. I tried to run too, but the bucket banged against my legs. "Wait, Mary!" I shouted.

My feet slipped on the steep ground. I dropped the bucket and berries spilled into the dirt. My knees felt like they were burning. I stared in horror at blood seeping through a hole in my stocking.

I scooped up some of the berries. My eyes blurred with tears. I began to run again. The trees seemed to grow taller and darker, as though they were squeezing me. Suddenly the forest was alive with crackling and rustling noises.

I thought, Wolves and bears! Wolves and bears!

I ran, gasping for air. Mary was waiting a little ways down the trail, sitting on the fallen tree. She looked at me and then she took the bucket.

She said sulkily, "It was just a joke. Don't tell Ma."

By then I was crying hard. I didn't say anything. I tried to wipe my face on my sleeve. It made smudgy wet marks.

We walked silently back to the cabin. Ma washed the cut on my knee where I had fallen. Max watched, his eyes round.

"It's more of a scrape than a cut," said Ma. She thought I was crying because I had hurt myself.

After supper, Ma made jam with the strawberries. She gave me two gleaming jars. "Put them in your trunk. They'll be nice next winter for you and Max and your papa."

Ma sounded so sure that Papa was coming back. If only I could be sure too. I went outside and looked at the empty brown road.

There wasn't a breath of wind. Then I heard a strange noise — an eerie howling that made goosebumps prickle the back of my neck. The dog growled from the shadows.

The noise came again. I shivered.

The cabin door opened. "Wolves," said Mary triumphantly. She stood very close to me. "I told you there were wolves. Does it make you afraid?"

"No," I lied.

"Me neither," said Mary. "I'm not afraid of anything."

I heard the wolves one more time. Then I went inside. That night, I buried myself deep inside the quilt. I put my hands over my ears. I tried not to think of Papa.

Chapter 8
Chores

Swish, swish, swish.

Mary pounded the dasher up and down in the butter churn.

"Do you know," she said in a loud, important voice, "that I milked Celery, gathered the eggs and emptied the pail of ashes all before breakfast?"

Up and down, up and down, went the

dasher in Mary's strong arms.

Swish, swish, swish.

Lazy, lazy, lazy. That's what it seemed to say to me. My cheeks burned.

"Trevor and Max have been picking rocks in the field for days," Mary went on. "It's not fair, Ma. Ellie doesn't do her share."

"Hush, Mary," said Ma. She was kneading bread dough at the wooden table. Her big hands slapped the soft mound.

I bit my lip. Making butter didn't look hard. "I'll take my turn now," I said nervously.

But when I took the handle, I felt clumsy. After a few minutes my arms ached.

"In England," I stammered, "we bought our butter from Edward the milkman."

Mary clicked her tongue. "Ma, that's all she talks about. England!"

I bent over the butter churn. I squeezed my eyes to keep the tears in. The cabin was quiet except for the thump of Ma's hands on the dough.

"Let me finish then," said Mary in an impatient voice. She worked the paddle

up and down with firm strokes. She began
to sing.

> *Come, butter, come.*
> *Come, butter, come.*
> *Peter standing at the gate*
> *Waiting for a butter cake*
> *Come, butter, come.*

Mary stopped churning. "There," she
said. "Done."

She glanced at Ma. Ma was bent over
the bake kettle, lifting out a loaf of warm,
yeasty bread.

Mary gave me a long, cold look. The
look said, "And with no help from you!"

That afternoon Mary brought the kittens
outside. She carried them in her apron skirt.
She sat down in the shade of the wild cherry
tree and spilled them gently onto the ground.

For a minute, five furry balls huddled
in the grass. Five stick tails twitched back

and forth. Then the kittens began to explore. The little black kitten batted his paw at a stalk of grass. A gray and white kitten crouched and pounced at a stick. He made tiny growling noises in his throat and rolled over and over.

The kittens bounded and crawled and skittered over the ground. When they got too far away, Mary lifted them up and brought them back.

I sat on my stump and swung my feet. Ma had given me some gray wool for knitting and had got me started. I was knitting a scarf for Papa. I bent over the needles. I pretended not to see Mary.

Mary lay down on her back. A kitten clambered up onto her tummy. She giggled and gave me a sideways look.

I frowned and counted stitches. Max and Trevor were playing with pebbles in the dirt at the side of the road. They had lined them up into two armies and were planning their war happily.

Click, click, click went my needles. Ma

had said that by the time I finished the scarf, Papa would surely be back. Click, click, click. I wished I could knit as fast as Ma.

After a few minutes, I rested my fingers. I looked up. Mary's eyes were closed. Four fuzzy balls curled up in her apron, their tummies panting up and down, their tiny motors humming.

Pirate was investigating a bucket. He stood on his back feet and reached up with his front paws. He tried to poke his chin over the rim. Clang! The bucket clattered over. Pirate leaped sideways. He braced his feet and hissed.

I laughed. I put down my knitting and rescued Pirate. His strong body squirmed in my hands. Then he tipped his face up and licked my cheek with his rough tongue.

"Give him to me," said Mary behind me. Her voice was cool. "I'm taking them back now."

I watched Mary carry the kittens to the barn, holding her apron in front of her like a basket.

I thought, I don't care.

But I did. When I held Pirate, I didn't miss Papa so much.

Chapter 9
Stuck Like Molasses

I pulled my shawl over my shoulders and stepped outside. For once, I was awake before Mary. I glanced back at the cabin and then ran across the yard to the henhouse.

The henhouse was dark and full of soft rustling sounds. A hen squawked softly. "Shh," I said.

I took a big breath. I closed my eyes

and stuck my hand under the smallest hen. I felt soft feathers and scratchy straw and then — a smooth, warm egg! I slid the egg out and laid it carefully in my basket.

I worked my way from hen to hen, until my basket was heavy with speckled brown eggs. There was one big old hen I left to the end. My secret name for her was Grandmother because she had sharp eyes and a disapproving stare. Quickly I slipped my hand into her nest. I pulled out the biggest egg of all.

Was it only a few weeks ago that I had been so afraid of hens? Smiling, I hurried back to the cabin. I couldn't wait to see the surprise on Mary's face.

Mary was setting the table for breakfast. Her cheeks were pink. "Pa's going to town," she said. "He's going to get the calico Ma ordered. He'll be gone for two days."

I set my basket of eggs carefully on the table. I couldn't understand why Mary was so excited. The town was just a scraggly row of cabins with a store at one end and a church at the other.

"Last time he brought me new hair ribbons," said Mary. "And peppermint sticks for everybody!"

I started to say, "In England ... " and then I bit my tongue.

Mary set a jug of milk on the table. She said, "I heard Pa tell Ma he's going to ask around about your Papa. See if anyone's heard anything."

I stared at Mary. I forgot about the eggs. My heart started to thump. Then I remembered Mrs. Robertson's hateful words about settlers getting lost in the wilderness.

I felt excited and scared at the same time.

It was the hottest day so far. After Pa left, Ma let the fire in the stone fireplace go out. She baked bread all morning in the outdoor oven. The chickens made little spurts of dust when they scratched for grubs. After a while, they settled on the ground like soft red pillows. The yellow dog lay in a patch of shade with his tongue hanging out.

In the afternoon, Ma plucked the big gray goose that lived in the chicken yard. She pulled a woollen work sock over its head and clamped its squirming body between her knees.

Mary and Trevor and Max and I sat in the shade under the cherry tree and watched.

"Do you remember the time Papa brought the duck home?" I said to Max.

"I don't remember," said Max.

"You must remember. Papa said he would build it a house but Grandmother made him take it away."

Max stuck his chin out. "I don't re-member!" He squirmed away from me. He was watching Ma. His face wrinkled with worry. "Do you think the goose hurts?"

"No," said Mary. "It doesn't hurt at all. He's just a silly old goose for complaining so much."

Trevor leaped up. His face was red

and his eyes bright. He hung a sack over his head and raced in circles, flapping his arms. "Honk! Honk! Honk! I'm a silly old goose."

Mary screamed with laughter. Max clapped his hands. He chased after Trevor.

"Honk! Honk! Honk!" he yelled joyfully. "I'm a silly old goose too!"

The yellow dog barked. A scraggly red chicken ran squawking into the long grass, clucking furiously.

"Goodness," said Ma, but she was smiling.

I felt myself smile too. Part of me wanted to run like a goose too. But my feet were stuck to the ground, like molasses in the bottom of a jug.

Trevor collapsed in a heap on the dusty ground. He lay very still. Mary leaned over him and pulled off the sack. "He's just pretending, Ma!" she shouted. "He's laughing!"

"Do it again!" cried Max, but Trevor shook his head. He was breathing hard and his forehead glistened with sweat.

Mary picked up the sack. She draped it over her shoulders. She paraded back and forth. "I am a great lady from England," she said.

"There," said Ma. She let the goose go. Max ran to Ma and threw himself on her lap. They hugged in a cloud of downy feathers. I thought that Ma probably felt like a big pillow.

I heard Max say, "If Papa comes back, do we have to leave?"

Everything went still inside me. *When* Papa comes back, I wanted to shout. *When* Papa comes back.

A hard lump filled my throat. I knelt beside Mary and helped her fill the sack with the soft gray feathers.

Chapter 10
The Storm

That night, I woke up to a terrible roaring noise. It was the wind, howling outside the cabin walls. Ma was standing beside our bed.

"Trevor is sick," she said. Mary sat up beside me. She stared at Ma. Then she quickly climbed out of bed. I followed, fuzzy with sleep.

Ma had lit the lamps, but the windows were black with the night. She had moved Trevor into the bedroom. Trevor looked small lying in Ma and Pa's big bed. His hair was mussed and two red spots burned in his cheeks. "Ma!" he cried. "Where are you?"

"I'm here, lamb."

One minute Trevor was shivering, the next, he was tossing and turning and pushing the blankets away.

"It's the fever," said Ma. She made Trevor drink a tonic. She said it was made from wild black cherry bark steeped in whiskey. Trevor made a face when he drank it. It must have tasted terrible.

Mary and I fetched water in a pail from the barrel outside. The wind screamed like a wild animal. It grabbed at our nighties. The tops of the trees swayed back and forth in a strange dance. A bucket clattered across the yard. I was glad to go back inside the cabin and shut out the storm.

I dipped a cloth in the cool water and

carried it to Ma. She wiped Trevor's face. His eyes were like dark round stones. His face glistened with sweat. Mary reached out and touched Trevor's hand. "He's burning, Ma!" she hissed.

Crash! A terrible noise shook the cabin. We stared at each other. Then Mary and I ran to the window.

Mary cried, "The cherry tree! It's down!"

I pressed my face against the glass. I could see a great shadowy shape like a black monster stretching across the yard. The branches looked like long arms reaching out to the cabin. Goosebumps prickled the back of my neck.

Max called for me, his voice thin with fright. I wrapped him in the quilt from his bed and settled him beside the fireplace.

Trevor began to cry. "I'm hot, Ma!" he gasped between sobs.

Mary and I took turns carrying the cloth back and forth for Ma. It was cool when I dipped it in the pail and hot and sticky when Ma gave it back to me. After a long time, Trevor stopped crying. He lay like a pale ghost, his eyes shut. Once he called out something, but it was a jumble of mixed-up words. I looked at Mary. Her eyes were wide and frightened.

Then a loud drumming noise filled my ears. Rain. The wind beat the raindrops against the window, making a rattling noise like pebbles. Suddenly my eyelids felt heavy and my arms and legs like thick cotton. I huddled in a chair beside Max and tried to shut out the pounding rain and the shrieking wind.

I must have slept for a while because when I woke up, everything was still. Max was asleep, curled up on the floor like one of Mary's kittens. There was no noise outside and the cabin was filled with a pale light. I went to the window and looked out. A round full moon floated in the black sky.

I watched it for a minute. Was Papa, somewhere, looking at the moon too? Then

I went into the bedroom. Ma was holding Trevor's hand. Mary stood beside the bed. Her face was streaked with dried tears. Her nightie was crumpled and her hair had fallen out of its braid.

"We need the doctor," said Ma. "If only your Pa were here …"

I stared at Ma. The doctor's cabin was four miles down the road, the way Papa and Max and I had come. Four miles through the woods.

After a long time, Mary whispered, "I can't, Ma. Not by myself."

I could feel my heart hammering in my chest. I took a big breath.

"I'll go with you," I said.

Mary and I slipped into our dresses and stockings. We didn't talk at all. I was shivering so much it was hard to lace my boots. Then Mary opened the cabin door. The yard was bathed in moonlight. The wet branches of the cherry tree glistened like silver. Big drops of water dripped off the edge of the cabin roof.

I looked up the road. Where it made a bend, it looked like it was swallowed up by the shadowy forest. I wanted Ma to say, "Don't go." But she was singing softly to Trevor.

"Come on," said Mary. Her voice shook. There were two red circles on her pale cheeks. We began to run.

Chapter 11
Wolf!

Mud splashed on our stockings. The trees made tall skinny shadows across the road. Big round puddles shone in the moonlight. There were pieces of branches everywhere that had blown around in the storm.

We ran past Pa's fields. Then the road dipped back into the forest. It was alive with little sounds, cracklings and rustlings and dripping leaves. I was sure it was full of fierce animals.

We came to an old dead tree that Papa and I had passed. It was still standing, but it had a great split down the middle. I remembered Papa saying that if trees could talk, that tree would have stories to tell. All that seemed such a long time ago now.

A cramp stabbed at the side of my stomach. "I have to walk," I told Mary. I tried to keep my eyes straight ahead. I thought, Don't look at the forest. I counted my steps to one hundred.

I looked sideways at Mary. Tears were slipping down her cheeks. I said in a loud voice, "In England, peppermints grow on trees."

Mary's mouth dropped open. "They do?"

"Oh, yes. And horses can talk." I was smiling. Slowly, Mary smiled too.

"Chickens lay golden eggs," I said.

"I know one!" shouted Mary. "Houses are made out of sugar! Oh, I wish I lived in England!"

We both laughed at that.

"In England," I said at last, "I never had a best friend."

Mary smiled hard then. She took my hand.

We began to run again.

How far had we gone? One mile? Two miles? Nothing on the road looked familiar now. Papa had pointed out the doctor's cabin when we had passed it. But it had been dark and closed up. What if no one was there now? I felt scared when I thought of Trevor's still, white face.

We walked ten steps and ran ten steps, sucking in big gulps of air.

I said, "My stomach hurts."

Mary squeezed my hand harder. "Mine too," she gasped.

The mud soaked through our stockings and splattered the hems of our dresses. I thought about Grandmother saying, "The wilderness is no place for a girl."

Once Mary said, "Do you think Trevor...?"

"He'll be all right," I said in a much braver voice than I felt.

Ten steps … and then ten more. I could hear Mary breathing hard beside me.

Suddenly a dark shape slid out of the trees in front of us.

It had thick gray fur and a pointed face like a dog.

"A wolf!" hissed Mary. She grabbed my shoulder. I felt like I was frozen to the ground. The wolf stood in the middle of the road, staring at us with yellow eyes. Then it gave one sharp bark and slipped back into the forest.

"Run!" shouted Mary. My chest felt hollow and my arms and legs turned to ice. I ran hard, not caring about the pain in my stomach. My heart pounded wildly and a roaring noise filled my head.

After what seemed like ages, we stopped. We sucked in big gulps of air. Was the wolf gone?

We looked into the dark forest. Mary gave a frightened gasp. The wolf was

sliding along in the shadows without making any noise at all. It was following us! I felt dizzy with fear.

We ran hard, our boots splashing on the ground. We came to a bend in the road, and there at last was the doctor's cabin. There was a warm yellow light in the window. Just a few more steps. I screamed at myself to hurry, hurry, hurry!

Mary's breath was coming out in little choking sobs. My legs felt as wobbly as porridge. I looked back, and I saw the wolf's yellow eyes gleaming in the darkness. Then it turned and melted into the trees.

Mary banged on the cabin door.

Chapter 12
Papa

The doctor's wife gave us hot, sugary tea and a thick slice of bread and honey to stay us on the ride home. The doctor hitched up his wagon. He talked in a soothing voice to his horse, who pawed the ground uneasily.

The doctor had to drive slowly because of the puddles and the fallen branches. I huddled close to Mary. She was shivering.

"I'm so glad you came with me," she whispered. "The wolf — it's the first one I ever saw."

I looked at Mary, surprised.

"I was scared to death," she admitted.

"Me too," I said.

We were quiet for the rest of the ride. By the time we got home, the sky was turning pale blue. I was glad to see that it was morning. I thought the long night would never end.

The cow Celery was bellowing in the field. She sounded mournful. Mary and I brought her to the barn and took turns milking her.

Mary was very stern with Celery. "You have to let her know who's the boss," she explained.

I was clumsier than Mary, and Celery kept turning her big head around to stare at me with her sad brown eyes.

But Mary said, "That's better than *my* first try."

After a while, Max ran out to the barn, full of news. "The doctor is giving Trevor medicine. He doesn't want it. Ma is crying."

Mary bit her lip. She looked frightened. I told Max to hush. I poured some of the milk into the kittens' bowl and we watched them drink. Then I showed Max how to make Pirate leap in the air for a wisp of hay. Mary waited quietly. I knew she was thinking about Trevor.

After a long time, we heard the yellow dog bark and the doctor's horse whinny. We ran outside. A wagon rumbled around the bend in the road. It was traveling quickly, the wheels splashing through the puddles.

Mary's breath came out in a whoosh. "It's your papa," she cried.

I froze for a second. Then Papa stood up, pulling the reins. Beside me, Max shrieked.

I flew over the ground. Papa leaped off the wagon and swept me into his arms.

"Me too," shouted Max, running, and

Papa hugged us both.

I couldn't stop staring at Papa. He looked so different. His face was brown and he had grown a bushy beard. But when he smiled, his eyes were the same.

The questions spilled out of Max. "Did you find our land? Did you build a cabin? Why were you so long?"

Papa laughed. "One thing at a time! Our land is just over a day's wagon ride from here. I have been busy cutting down trees and building a shanty." He smiled at me. "The cabin will be built soon."

My heart thumped. I wasn't thinking of the cabin. Papa said our land was not too far away. Mary and I could stay best friends.

"There is a lake," said Papa. "We will build our cabin right beside it."

"Does the lake have a name?" said Mary. "Ellie likes to give things names."

Papa considered. "We must ask the Indians. They have a camp on the opposite shore."

Indians! I shivered.

"I'm not afraid of Indians," said Mary in a loud voice.

"I should hope not," said Papa. He ruffled Max's hair.

I felt dizzy with happiness. Then the cabin door opened. The doctor stepped into the sunshine. He nodded at Papa.

Beside me, I heard Mary suck in her breath. I squeezed her hand hard.

The doctor said, "The lad's fever has broken." His face broke into a wide smile. "He is going to be fine."

"Ellie! Look at me!" shouted Max.

Max was standing on the top rail of the fence. His arms stuck out like a bird's wings. He jumped to the ground. He stood up and dusted off his knees.

I took a big breath. I climbed to the top of the fence. I tried to straighten my legs, but my knees wobbled like jelly. I grinned at Mary and Max.

I could see far down the road where

Mary and I had run in the night. The road looked different in the sunshine. I wondered where the wolf had gone.

Then I looked the other way. The road disappeared into the forest. Somewhere down that road was our homestead.

"Jump!" shouted Max.

I jumped. Whoosh! The ground rushed up to meet me and I landed with a thump.

I smiled up at Mary. "Tell Trevor," I said.

Mary nodded. Trevor was sleeping. The doctor had said that he needed a lot of rest. Papa and Max and I would be gone when Trevor woke up.

Mary's Pa had come home the night before. He had brought new hair ribbons — red for Mary and yellow for me — and whistles for Max and Trevor. He helped Papa load our trunks in the wagon.

Max looked sad. Papa said, "Ma has enough to do looking after Trevor without looking after us anymore. It's time we got started on our own cabin so we'll be ready for the winter."

Mary had a surprise for me, hidden in her apron. Pirate!

"For me?" I said. "For keeps?"

"Yes," said Mary.

"In England," I said, "I had a cat. But only for one day."

Max hugged Ma hard. "I will miss you!" he cried.

I hugged Ma next. She felt like a soft pillow. She smelled like flowers and warm bread. Then Max and I climbed up on the wagon seat beside Papa. I cuddled Pirate against my chest. My heart was beating like a bird's wings with excitement.

Inside me was a bit of sadness too. I wondered when I would see Mary again.

"Goodbye, Max. Goodbye, Ellie from England," said Pa in his rumbling voice.

"Ellie from Canada," I said firmly.

Papa clucked to Billy and George. I waved to Mary.

Then we set off for our new home.

BECKY CITRA is a primary school teacher who lives in the small community of Bridge Lake, British Columbia. Her home is a ranch with eight horses, a Springer spaniel named Robin, and a cat named Cookie. She also shares the property with frequent visitors: bears, moose and coyotes. When Becky is not teaching or working on her ranch, she loves to read and write stories for children. She is the author of two other children's novels, *My Homework is in the Mail* and *School Campout*. She is also working on a sequel to *Ellie's New Home*.

Also in the *Orca Young Reader* series:

Phoebe and the Gypsy
Andrea Spalding

Phoebe Hiller's visit to her grandmother's cottage
in England is not going well. All the people in the
village know who she is and fuss over her
"foreign" accent and manners. She's treated like
an alien every time she opens her mouth. It's
enough to make a regular Canadian kid feel like a
circus act.

But one day Phoebe meets a Gypsy, a
mysterious woman who seems to know *all* about
her — including the secret that Phoebe has kept
from the whole world. And now everything is
changed.

Also in the *Orca Young Reader* series:

Three On Three
Eric Walters

Nick and Kia, the two best basketball players in
their grade, are eager to join up for the school's
"Three on Three" tournament. But they'll have to
play against the older grades as well. So there's
only one thing to do if they have any chance to
win — find an older kid to join their team.
Marcus, who is two grades above them and the
best player in the school, is the perfect choice.

Of course, Nick and Kia have to convince
Marcus to join them. And the two friends also
have to avoid becoming targets for the older kids
who also want Marcus on their team. This
tournament is going to be a lot more tricky than
they thought.

Also in the *Orca Young Reader* series:

The Keeper and the Crows
Andrea Spalding

A young boy visits his aunt for the summer only
to find himself in the middle of a fantastic
adventure. Aunt Dora is the "Keeper," protector of
a box full of terrible evil. The crows have stolen
the key and are now determined to take the box
as well. Somehow the boy must help his aunt
retrieve the key and outwit the crows, before they
steal the box and spill its secrets into an
unsuspecting world.

Also in the *Orca Young Reader* series:

Jesse's Star
Ellen Schwartz

A school assignment sends Jesse up to the attic to search out clues about his ancestors. But a reluctant Jesse finds more than he bargained for in his great-great-great-grandfather's traveling case. Whether he likes it or not, Jesse is about to take a journey back to Russia at the thenthe the century as he becomes Yossi, a boy determined to help his family escape to a new world.